Gus Gets Mad

Gus Gets Mad

by Frank Remkiewicz

Cartwheel
B·O·O·K·S®

SCHOLASTIC INC.
New York   Toronto   London   Auckland
Sydney   Mexico City   New Delhi   Hong Kong

For Jack

Copyright © 2011 by Frank Remkiewicz

All rights reserved. Published by Scholastic Inc.
SCHOLASTIC, CARTWHEEL BOOKS, and associated logos are trademarks and/or registered trademarks of Scholastic Inc.
Lexile is a registered trademark of MetaMetrics, Inc.

Library of Congress Cataloging-in-Publication Data is available.

ISBN 978-0-545-34252-0

18 17 16 15 14 13   16/0

Printed in the U.S.A.   40
First printing, October 2011

Gus goes to the park.

There is a sandbox!

He will have a good day.

Gus digs a hole.

A big hole.

Gus gets water.

He makes a lake.

A big lake.

The lake is not full.

He needs more water.

There is NO WATER!

Gus gets mad.

Very mad.

This is not a good day.

It is time to go.

Gus gets his toys.

Wow!

"My lake!" he says.

Gus had a good day.

A very good day.